# THE SEED

## WHAT SHALL I GROW UP TO BE?

# MICHAEL R. LOSEY

ISBN: 149228288X
ISBN 13: 9781492282884
Library of Congress Control Number: 2013916031
CreateSpace Independent Publishing Platform

## For parents, grandparents, teachers and others

Like *The Seed*, each child, sooner or later, will wonder what he or she shall grow up to be. This book broaches that question and allows not only the reader but parents, grandparents, teachers and others to assist children with this very important question.

To aid in the value of the book's content, and to allow an additional teaching experience, this book is also available as a computer presentation. These programs offer several additional advantages such as:

- Unlike requiring a child or children to sit by the reader to see a book and its illustrations, the reader may elect to read the article from a computer. The book's optional presentations could even be linked to available media projection for classroom and other use.
- Today's computer savvy children could also watch or read the story by themselves with relative ease and at their own initiative.

Also use of the presentation format allows children to add to or change the book as their creative minds suggest. For instance, after reading the story, an 11 year old girl in our family wrote a song about The Seed. Other possibilities are:

- While most children books are written with the main character a male, this book is intentionally gender neutral. Thus the child reader could make the Seed a "He" or " She," and/or give the Seed a name.
- The reader could creatively change the story.
- Illustrations could be changed. They could also be animated allowing some art work to be programmed to appear when the reader "clicks" after or before reading a page.

For a complimentary computer based copy of THE SEED see the following website: **www.thebooktheseed.com**. On that website you can select your desired format. You will be asked to confirm that you have purchased *The Seed* and where as well as pledge that you will not further distribute the presentation(s) without permission. (Note: Teachers may distribute to their students without restriction.) If you have not yet purchased the book, you can order it at **www. createspace or amazon.com**.

## CHAPTER 1
# BEING BORN

Could this be what they call spring? It had been very cold for such a long time and now it was slowly growing warm. With the warmth also came rain instead of snow, longer days and shorter nights. The birds were returning and all of nature was awakening. The seed thought *'This must be spring'.*

The seed had lain silent for a long time awaiting the right moment. Just as a baby duck knows how to swim and baby birds know how to fly, a seed knows how to grow, and spring was the time for many things to begin life.

As the heat from the sun warmed the soil, and the water from the rain gave the seed strength, the seed reached out. The soil welcomed the seed and grasped it firmly. The soil fed the seed and the seed grew larger.

Then one day, the seed broke through the soil and was born.

Birth for a seed is very much like birth for other living things.

The seed was born very small, weak, and unprotected, but most of all the seed wondered who it was.

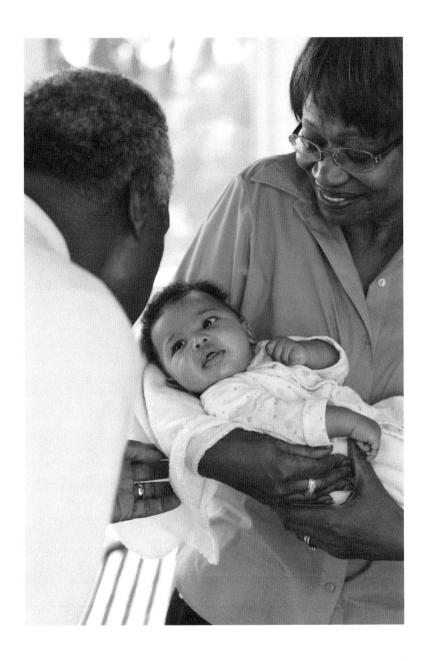

Fortunately, most birds, animals, and children have mothers, fathers, grandparents or someone else to help them learn the answers to these important questions.

However, a seed is one of the few living things sent into the world by its parents to grow wherever the winds blow it; or birds carry it; the soil will receive it; the sun will warm it and water will feed it.

This is why we find trees, flowers and other things living together everywhere.

It was for these reasons that the seed wondered where and who it could be.

## CHAPTER 2
# THE FOREST

Now born, the seed looked about and it could see many living things.

It saw a covering of grass, flowers of different shapes and colors, bushes and shrubs.

Most of all, the seed noticed the tall trees stretching high into the sky.

You see, a seed cannot determine what type of seed it will be, for that is already decided once one is a seed. Again, just like you and me, a seed can wonder what it will grow up to be.

The seed soon knew it was not merely grass because it quickly grew much thicker and taller.

Surely, the seed was not a flower, because it was not as pretty as a flower should be. Could it be lucky enough to be a tree? They grew so tall they seemed to scrape the sky.

Trees danced with the wind and caught the first rain. They were so strong and spread their branches so wide that they protected the rest of the forest lying below.

Yes, the little seed would like to be a tree.

## CHAPTER 3
# THE FIRST FALL

Although the seed grew rapidly that first spring and summer, soon it was cool again and the flowers had disappeared. Just as soon as they had disappeared, the trees' green leaves turned to many different colors, giving the forest a new type of beauty.

At the same time, the seed had grown to such a size that it now had branches, and on its branches were leaves. But the seed thought its leaves were funny-looking. They were straight and narrow and dark green in color.

The seed had no flowers on its branches, nor had its leaves changed to beautiful colors, like the other trees. Instead, the seed's leaves seemed as though they would stay forever green.

Soon even the trees' beautiful leaves fell to the ground. The trees were still tall and strong, but now they were undressed.

Indeed, as the winter came and the snow fell, the seed was the only one who kept its leaves.

Possibly something was wrong. Why was the seed so very different from the other trees in the forest?

As it snowed, the seed stood alone, still wondering who it was as its branches became a white coat.

## CHAPTER 4
# SPRING AGAIN

Spring came again, much as the seed remembered it. New seeds were born and all things started to grow once more. The seed also grew. Now the seed was taller than many of the other living things in the forest but of course, so much smaller than the big trees.

As the seed grew taller, it also grew wider. So wide, in fact, it soon noticed it was almost as wide as it was tall.

'*Surely, now I know,*' thought the seed sadly, '*I am not a tree.*'

Then one day, the silence of the forest was broken by workers walking about, carefully studying the bushes and trees.

They carried little red ribbons that they placed on some of the bushes and trees. It seemed they were placing the ribbons on as many of the forest's living things as possible.

The seed thought the ribbons were pretty and wondered if it would get one and what they were for.

A few days later, a truck appeared carrying a large bulldozer. Soon the bulldozer was at work carefully clearing a portion of the forest.

The seed noticed that the trees and bushes with the red ribbons were not being removed.

It thought, *'Will I be taken from the forest?'*

Then, the big bulldozer came directly toward the spot where the seed had grown into what it was. Just before the blade of the bulldozer would have pushed the seed aside, the big machine stopped. From it stepped a large man who called to another man, *"Gee, boss, do you really think we should take this thing out of here?"*

"It's O.K. to let it stand," answered the boss. "*Put a red ribbon on it for now. We want to keep as much of the forest as we can before we start building homes. We will let the new owners decide.*"

'*The new owners! Who are the new owners?*' thought the seed. '*And what is to happen to me?*'

The seed did not have to wait long to learn what was happening.

Soon there were many people looking in the forest for a good place to build a home for their family.

One family examined the part of the forest where the seed stood.

When the workman asked if the family wanted to remove the Seed, they said, "*No*" and that they would decide what to do with it later.

## CHAPTER 5
# THE NEW OWNERS

By this time it was growing cold again. Some of the trees were gone, so each tree that remained tried to display extra fall beauty.

The family's house was complete and they were able to move into their new home just before the first snow.

This seemed to be a busy and happy time for everyone. People came and went carrying different colored packages with bows on top.

'It must be someone's birthday', thought the seed.

The snow brought the children out to play. There was a girl and her little brother. They seemed to pay no attention to the seed as the seed stood there watching them play. If the seed were a flower, they would have admired it, or if it had been a tall tree, they might have climbed it.

But, 'No', thought the seed. 'What would the children want with a short squat thing like me?

Then one day, the children came out to where the seed stood. They looked at it carefully as they had never done before.

They whispered to each other as though they thought the seed could hear them.

'*What were they going to do?*' worried the seed.

They were nice children. However, the seed worried they would pull and bend it because its limbs were not as strong as the big trees, and might break.

Then they left, only to quickly return with their father and mother. Their parents also looked at the seed and said, *"Yes, it will do just fine."*

'*Just fine for what?*' thought the seed.

But the seed didn't have to wait long to find out. Soon the children, along with their mother and father, gathered around. The father had brought a big box from the house. Inside the box were beautiful treasures.

First, there was a star that they placed on the seed's crown.

Then they wrapped a string of lights around and around. Finally, they hung beautiful ornaments, large and small, from the seed's branches.

As they finished, it grew dark, and they all stood back as though to admire their work.

Then the father asked, "Is everyone ready?"

When they all said, "Yes", the father turned on the lights that they had placed on the seed's limbs. There were many beautiful colors lighting up the branches and twinkling off the ornaments and the snow.

"It's beautiful" said the mother.

"It is our very own," said the boy.

"We will have it each year," assured the father.

Finally the little girl said, "It's the most beautiful Christmas tree in the whole world!"

"*A Christmas tree!*" heard the seed.

'*Can it be? Oh, what a privilege to be a Christmas tree!*'

Now at last, the seed knew what it was to be. Each year as it watched the passing seasons, the seed enjoyed the flowers of spring, the green grasses of summer, and the trees changing colors in the fall. Most of all every winter the seed awaited the opportunity to do what only it could do – ***Be a Christmas tree!***

ISBN 9781492282884

9 781492 282884

Made in the USA